THE DAY VERONICA WAS NOSY

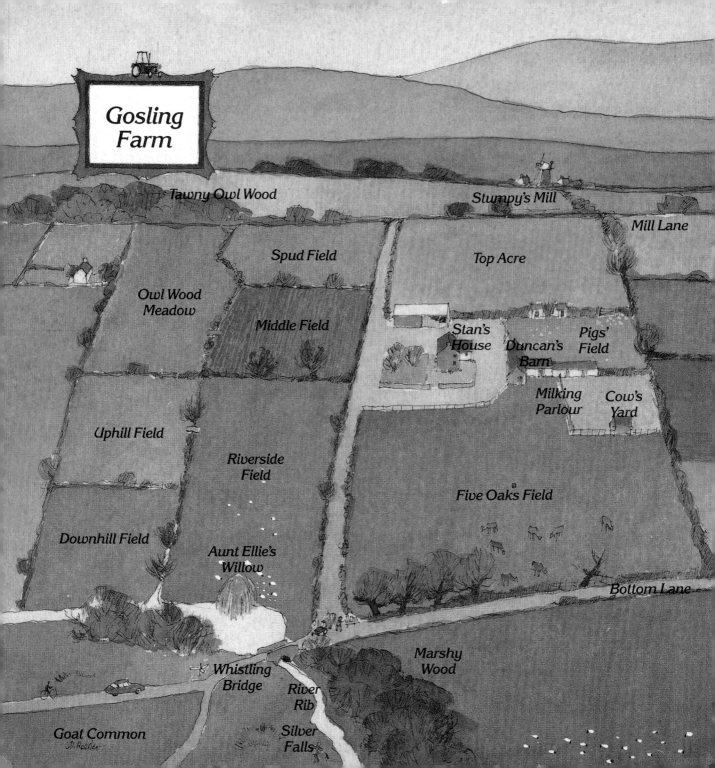

Wrigglesworth

Beech Farm

Walter's
Garage

Heronwood Lake

River Dean

For Kerrie

First published in Great Britain by
William Collins Sons & Co Ltd in 1990
First published in Picture Lions in 1992

Picture Lions is an imprint of the Children's Division,
part of HarperCollins Publishers Limited,
77-85 Fulham Palace Road, Hammersmith,
London W6 8JB

ISBN: 0 00 664188-1

Printed in Great Britain

A LITTLE RED TRACTOR BOOK

THE DAY VERONICA WAS NOSY

COLIN REEDER

Text by Elizabeth Laird

PictureLions

An Imprint of HarperCollins*Publishers*

The mother hen woke early on a windy autumn day on Gosling Farm. She peered through one black eye at the daylight, and squawked at it. She woke her sisters, who lifted their heads, shook their combs and cackled for their breakfast.

Duncan the tractor woke up too. His oil had settled in the night. He felt cold, and slow, and lazy.

"Morning all," said Stan, as he opened the barn doors. "Time for work, Duncan."

Stan jumped into the cab and turned on Duncan's engine. Duncan shook himself, coughed, spluttered and began to feel warmer.

"Good lad," said Stan.

Duncan's engine was running smoothly now. He was ready for work. Stan drove him out into the farmyard and fixed the trailer to the hook between Duncan's back wheels.

He piled some posts and wire into the trailer and threw in a bag of tools.

"Easy does it," he said, as he steered Duncan out into the lane.

Duncan chugged happily down to where the cows were grazing in Five Oaks field.

The cows raised their heads from the thick wet grass when they heard Duncan coming. They knew the little red tractor. He didn't bother them. They went back to their munching.

But Veronica, the youngest calf, wrinkled her nose and whisked her tail. Then she kicked up her heels and trotted over to see what was what.

Veronica was nosy.

Duncan stopped under a tree. Veronica stopped behind his rear wheels, and sniffed at Duncan's big black tyres. Stan got down and inspected the fence. Veronica inspected it too. Stan found a hole and Veronica found it too. Stan fetched his tools and a new fence post from the trailer. Veronica watched him.

"Out of my way, little 'un," he said. "I can't get on, with you under my feet all the time."

A puff of blustery wind blew a shower of yellow leaves out of the hedgerow, and Veronica darted off to watch them. Stan finished fixing the post, got back into Duncan's cab and drove up towards the next gap in the fence. Suddenly, the little calf bounced back again. She was nearly under Duncan's wheels!

"Oi, little rascal!" shouted Stan.

Duncan swerved, just in time. He missed Veronica, but he bumped into the old hollow oak tree in the hedgerow.

"Steady on!" said Stan.

He jumped out to inspect the damage.

"No harm done," he said.

Veronica inspected the damage too. She poked her nose into the old hollow tree and pawed at it with her sharp little hoof.

Whee! Buzz! A stream of short, fast, noisy things came shooting straight past her. Veronica jumped after them. She'd never seen hornets before. She didn't know they could sting.

Moo! Maroo!

The little calf jumped, bobbed her head up and down, lashed out with her hooves, and ran away across the field.

Stan ran up to her.

"Here, girl, what's up with you?" he said.

Veronica didn't hear him. Her nose hurt. A furious hornet had stung her!

She raced to the trough and plunged her sore nose into the water. Stan ran after her.

The hornets spotted him. They turned in mid-air and buzzed angrily. Stan took a step backwards.

"Oh dear, oh lor! Hornets!" he said.

He took another step backwards. The hornets came closer.

"Help!" shouted Stan and he ran as fast as he could.

Duncan was standing ready, with his cab door wide open. Stan jumped inside and shut it. There was glass all around him now. He was safe inside Duncan.

"Phew!" said Stan, and wiped his forehead. "Good thing you were here, Duncan. Those hornets can't get in here."

The hornets were still angry. They hated having their nest disturbed. It had taken them a year to build it. They flew round Duncan and buzzed. They settled on his long, red bonnet.

 They crawled all over his exhaust pipe

 and looked in through his windows.

They even tried to sting his tyres. Duncan didn't mind. He didn't feel a thing.

Stan started the engine with a roar. The hornets didn't like it. They hovered for a moment. Then they streamed away, past their old nest, over the water meadow and on up the river to build a new home by Heronwood Lake.

Veronica was still at the trough. Stan drove Duncan up to her and got down to take a look. She jumped a bit, but she let Stan touch her. She trusted Stan.

"Let's see your poor old nose, then," he said, and the calf licked his hand with her rough, pink tongue.

"Hm," said Stan. "Not too bad. Lucky you've got a good thick skin. You'll be better in no time, I'll be bound."

Veronica was feeling better already. She spotted a vole in the grass and bounded off to investigate. The vole ran near the hollow tree. Veronica stopped. She wouldn't go near that tree, not for a while, anyway.

Stan watched her, and laughed.

"She'll do," he said. Then he climbed back into the cab and patted the steering wheel. "Thank you, Duncan old lad. It's a good thing you were here. I'd have been in a right pickle without you."

He put Duncan into gear and the little tractor rumbled off over the field, his engine singing with happiness.

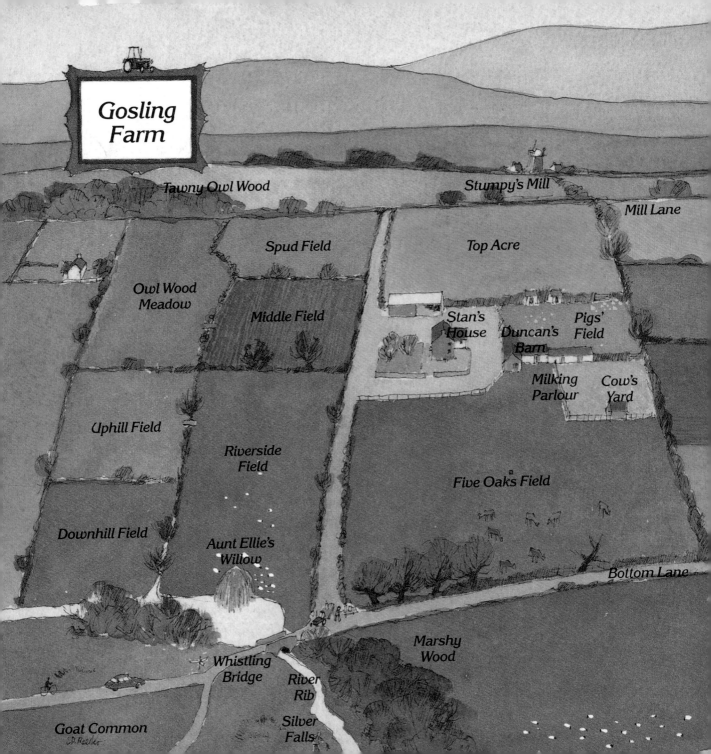

Gosling
Farm

Tawny Owl Wood

Stumpy's Mill

Mill Lane

Spud Field

Top Acre

Owl Wood
Meadow

Middle Field

Stan's
House

Duncan's
Barn

Pigs'
Field

Milking
Parlour

Cow's
Yard

Uphill Field

Riverside
Field

Five Oaks Field

Downhill Field

Aunt Ellie's
Willow

Bottom Lane

Whistling
Bridge

Marshy
Wood

River
Rib

Goat Common

Silver
Falls

Wrigglesworth

Beech Farm

Walter's
Garage

Heronwood Lake

River Dean